KT-432-169

Mara
the Meerkat
Fairy

by Daisy Meadows

ORCHARD

www.rainbowmagic.co.uk

The Fairyland Palace

Meadow

Stream

Beehive

Arctic Tundra

Eucalyptus Forest

Tropical Waterfall

Jack Frost's
Ice Castle

To Jack Frost's Zoo ⤴

Wild Woods
Nature
Reserve

Watering Hole

Pagoda

Desert Oasis

Jack Frost's Spell

I love animals, yes I do,
I want my very own private zoo!
I'll capture the animals one by one,
With fairy magic to help me on!

A koala, a tiger, an Arctic fox,
I'll keep them in cages with giant locks.
Every kind of animal will be there,
A panda, a meerkat, a honey bear.
The animals will be my property,
I'll be master of a huge menagerie!

Contents

A Very Tricky Task

"So, all we know about today's job is
that it's going to be particularly tricky!"
Kirsty Tate remarked to her best friend,
Rachel Walker, as they made their way
along a path through the woods.

The two girls had volunteered to spend
a week of the summer holidays working
as junior rangers at Wild Woods Nature
Reserve. "What do you think we'll be
doing, Rachel?"

"I don't know, but I'm looking forward to finding out when we meet Becky in the meadow!" Rachel replied with a grin. Becky was the head of the nature reserve. "I hope it's something we can do really well – and then we *might* just get another badge."

"I *love* getting badges," Kirsty said happily. She swung her backpack off her shoulders so she could proudly sneak a peek at the badges pinned to the pockets. This was the girls' third day at Wild Woods and they'd already won two badges because they'd managed to complete their tasks successfully on the previous two days.

The girls heard a rustling noise in the undergrowth and a little red squirrel scampered out of the bushes. He stopped in front of Rachel and Kirsty and gave them a cheeky glance.

"I heard what you were saying," the squirrel told them breathlessly. "And, you're right, you'll have a very difficult job to do today!" Then, giggling, he bounded away.

"Good luck!"
chirped a voice
from above.
The girls
looked up
and saw
a pair of
goldfinches
sitting on a branch

side by side. "Like the squirrel said,
you've got a very tricky task today."

"Very tricky!" the other goldfinch
agreed. Then the two birds soared up
into the blue sky.

"It's brilliant fun being able to talk
to animals!" Rachel exclaimed. "We
couldn't do it without the Baby Animal
Rescue Fairies' magic."

Kirsty nodded. "I just wish we hadn't

been given this magic for such a serious reason," she sighed. "We need the power to talk to animals so we can save wildlife everywhere from scary Jack Frost and his goblins!"

Rachel and Kirsty were in the middle of another thrilling fairy adventure. On their first day at Wild Woods, they'd met Bertram, the frog footman from Fairyland, who was visiting relatives at the nature reserve. At Bertram's invitation, the girls had been taken on a tour of the Fairyland Nature Reserve where they'd met the Baby Animal Rescue Fairies. These seven fairies were responsible for protecting animals in both the human and the fairy worlds with the help of the magical animal key rings clipped to their clothing.

Then Jack Frost and his goblins had arrived to spoil the girls' special day! Jack Frost had declared that he liked all the animals so much, he was going to collect one of each for his private zoo. He'd used his icy magic to steal the key rings and transfer them to his own belt. The girls had been horrified when Jack Frost had then handed the key rings to his goblins and sent them whizzing off to the human world, ordering them to bring back animals for his zoo.

The seven fairies were very upset, and the girls had offered their help. Immediately the fairies had combined their magic, giving Rachel and Kirsty the ability to talk to animals.

"So far we've met a baby panda and a tiger cub," Rachel reminded Kirsty

as they approached the meadow. "I
wonder if we'll meet another wild
animal today?"

"There's Becky," Kirsty said, peering
across the meadow. "Look, Rachel, she's
got a wheelbarrow with her."

Becky saw the girls
and waved.

"Becky's
not alone
in the
meadow!"
Rachel
said with
a grin, and
she pointed
at a rabbit
hopping across
the grass.

"There's another rabbit over there!"
Kirsty exclaimed. "And there's another –
and another!"

By the time Rachel and Kirsty had
climbed over the stile into the meadow,
they'd already spotted eight rabbits
hopping around. Quickly the girls ran to
join Becky. She was standing next to the
wheelbarrow and they saw it was full of
carrots, lettuces and cabbage leaves.

"Good morning, Rachel and Kirsty," Becky said, her eyes twinkling. "Your job for today is to count rabbits!"

Bunny Bother!

Rachel and Kirsty burst out laughing.

"I know it sounds silly," Becky went on, "but it's very helpful if we know the size of the rabbit population at Wild Woods. It means we can look after the environment and the animals properly."

She handed clipboards and pens to the girls. "Every time you see a rabbit, write it down," Becky went on. "You can use these veggies in the wheelbarrow to tempt the rabbits out of their warrens." And she pointed to the holes that the rabbits had dug in the meadow.

"We'll do our best," Kirsty promised.

"Good luck!" Becky told them. "I'll be back later to see how you're getting on." And she hurried off.

"There are lots of rabbits here!" Rachel remarked as a big brown bunny lolloped past them. "They're all different sizes, and some are black or brown."

"Some are just babies, too," Kirsty added. "I've got a feeling this is going to take us ages! Shall we count the bunnies in the field first?"

"Good idea," Rachel replied.

The girls ran around the meadow,
counting all the rabbits they could see
and keeping a tally on their clipboards.
It was hard work because the rabbits
wouldn't keep still and kept hopping
about all over the place.

"I wonder how many rabbits are in the warrens?" Rachel panted as she and Kirsty laid the carrots, lettuce and cabbage leaves on the grass in front of the holes. Then the girls stood by, clipboards at the ready. Soon furry heads began popping out of the warrens, and then rabbit after rabbit came hopping out, heading straight for the tasty vegetables.

"Ten, eleven, twelve!" Kirsty gasped as yet another rabbit scampered out of the burrow next to her. "There are loads of them, Rachel! And look, more are coming out of those holes that are a bit further away."

"I'll count those," Rachel suggested. "It'll be easier." And she hurried off a little way, murmuring, "Fourteen, fifteen, sixteen, seventeen…"

Kirsty didn't have a second to spare as she frantically counted the bunnies and then marked the number down on her clipboard. A short distance away, Rachel was doing the same. The vegetables were running out now, so Kirsty raced over to the wheelbarrow to grab some more.

The rabbits were munching away contentedly and Kirsty was counting under her breath when a small brown bunny hopped over to her.

"Excuse me," the bunny squeaked. "But have you counted *me* yet?"

"Yes, I just did," Kirsty laughed.

"Oh dear!" the rabbit sighed. "Your friend counted me already."

"Are you sure?" Kirsty asked, her heart sinking.

"Yes, she said I was number thirty-five!" the bunny replied.

Two more rabbits looked up from their lettuce leaves. "Your friend counted me already, too," one said.

"And me!" the other added.

"Oh no!" Kirsty groaned. She'd added these rabbits to her clipboard just a moment ago!

"Rachel?" Kirsty called, looking worried. "Some of the rabbits are telling me we've *both* counted them!"

"Yes, a rabbit has just told me the exact same thing," Rachel replied, rushing over to Kirsty.

The girls were dismayed, but they couldn't help giggling.

"This isn't just a tricky task!" Kirsty laughed. "It's impossible!"

"Should we start all over again?" asked Rachel.

25

"I think the same thing will happen again," Kirsty replied. "Maybe we need a better plan."

The girls watched the rabbits for a few moments, wondering how they could count them without getting in a muddle. Kirsty focused on one baby bunny who had a cute, fuzzy bit of fur sticking up on top of his head. The baby rabbit disappeared down a nearby hole.

Then, just seconds later, Kirsty gasped when the same rabbit popped out of a *different* hole a little further away.

"Rachel, I know why we've been getting confused!" Kirsty exclaimed. "I think the rabbits are going down one hole and then popping out of another. That's why we're counting them twice."

"I saw a TV programme about meerkats not long ago, and they lived underground in a maze of tunnels," Rachel said thoughtfully. "I bet these holes lead to lots of tunnels under the meadow, and *that's* how the bunnies can run around and pop in and out of different holes so easily."

Kirsty nodded. "We need a different way of counting them," she said, staring down at the rabbit burrow. It was then she noticed a misty golden glow around the entrance of the hole.

"I think I see fairy magic!" Kirsty announced excitedly, pointing at the glowing light.

The two girls raced over to investigate. As they reached the rabbit hole, a fairy fluttered out to greet them.

"Oh, hello, you're Mara the Meerkat Fairy!" Rachel gasped.

On Guard Against Goblins

Mara's anxious face broke into a smile. The little fairy wore a maroon and orange polka-dot skater dress with a narrow brown belt, leggings and flat purple Mary Jane shoes.

"Girls, I desperately need your help to protect a colony of my meerkats!" Mara cried. "The meerkat guards have spotted goblins near their burrow."

"Let's go right away!" Kirsty said. Quickly she and Rachel put their clipboards away in their backpacks. Mara was ready with her wand, and one sprinkling of magical fairy dust instantly whisked the three of them away from the nature reserve.

Just a few seconds later the girls found themselves standing on top of a huge sand dune, the burning sun beating down overhead from a cloudless sky. A vast

desert of dazzling orange sand stretched
out around them, and the only objects
Kirsty and Rachel could see were some
half-dead, leafless trees in the distance.

"I can't see any meerkats!" Rachel
began, turning around to look. But the
sand was slippery underfoot and she lost
her balance. Rachel gasped as she fell
backwards. Next moment she was sliding
down the slope on her bottom.

"That's one way to get down the sand dune, I suppose!" Mara laughed, fluttering after her.

Once Rachel had got over the shock, she started enjoying herself as she zoomed along, sending sand flying around her. Kirsty laughed as she sat down, too, and slid down the sandy slope behind Rachel.

Giggling, the girls landed in a heap at the bottom of the dune.

"Oh, that was great fun!" Rachel panted, standing up. "But now I'm really hot and thirsty."

"We've got water in our backpacks," Kirsty reminded her. "And sun cream."

"You'll need them to stay safe in this heat, girls," said Mara.

The girls drank some water, then they covered themselves with sun cream.

"That's better," Rachel remarked. "But I still can't see any meerkats!"

Mara laughed. "The desert is full of them," she replied. "Just use your eyes!"

The girls glanced around. They both caught sight of something moving in a hole in the sand and crept closer. Then a little furry head popped out.

"It's a baby meerkat!"
Kirsty exclaimed.

"Oh, she's
so cute!"
Rachel
breathed,
staring at the
meerkat's black-
ringed eyes and tiny black ears.

Suddenly the baby meerkat was
pulled gently back down the hole, and
two adult meerkats scampered out.
Immediately they sat up on their back
legs and began scanning the desert all
around them. Then the girls saw the
baby meerkat poke her head out again.
She waved and smiled at Rachel and
Kirsty, her dark eyes bright and playful.
The girls were enchanted.

"Isn't she gorgeous?" Kirsty said as she and Rachel smiled and waved back.

"Girls, meet Missy, short for Mischief!" Mara said, pointing her wand at the baby meerkat. "And these two are our brave meerkat guards."

"We're glad to see you, Mara," one of the guards squeaked. "There have been some *very* strange green creatures with big feet wandering around the desert."

Rachel glanced knowingly at Kirsty. *Goblins!*

"The other meerkats are staying underground out of sight until those funny green animals have gone," the other guard added. "We really don't like them!"

Just then the girls heard noises in the distance. The meerkat guards heard them too, and their whiskers started twitching nervously.

The noises were coming closer, and Kirsty could make out the sound of loud, gruff voices.

"Goblins!" she gasped.

Squeaking with anxiety, the meerkat guards dived for the hole and disappeared down it with Missy.

"Girls, let's try to stop the goblins coming any closer," Mara whispered, flying to hide beneath Kirsty's sun hat.

Swiftly, Rachel and Kirsty hurried across the sand in the direction of the voices. Then they saw three goblins wearing bright green shorts, shirts and large sun hats stagger over the top of a nearby dune. They all looked sweaty and exhausted.

"I'm too hot!" the smallest goblin wailed dismally.

"Stop complaining!" the biggest goblin retorted. "We can go as soon as we've found a meerkat to take with us."

"But where *are* the meerkats?" asked the third goblin, who had extra-large ears. "We haven't seen any yet."

As the girls approached the goblins, Rachel exclaimed under her breath and clutched Kirsty's arm. "Look at the biggest goblin's shorts!" she whispered.

Kirsty stared at the side pocket of the goblin's shorts, and Mara peeped out from her hiding place to take a look, too. They could see a small, furry meerkat toy sticking out.

"That's my magical key ring!" Mara murmured with a smile.

"Good! Now we know exactly where it is," Kirsty said. "But how do we get it back?"

Missy Makes Mischief!

The goblins trudged on through the sand, grumbling loudly about the heat. When they reached the girls, they stopped.

"Are there meerkats around here?" the smallest goblin asked hopefully.

Kirsty laughed. "There are no meerkats in the desert!" she replied with a grin.

"The only meerkat around here is that cute little toy," Rachel remarked casually, pointing at Mara's key ring poking out of the goblin's pocket.

The biggest goblin groaned and took off his hat to wipe his sweaty green brow. The other two did the same, and that gave Kirsty an idea.

"It's really hot, isn't it?" she said sympathetically. "Don't you have any water to cool down?"

"We did but we drank it all," the smallest goblin replied.

"Well, Rachel and I have plenty," Kirsty said. She took a bottle of water from her rucksack, and so did Rachel. The goblins stared greedily at the bottles, licking their lips. "We'll trade you a drink of our water for that toy you have in your pocket. Deal?"

"Deal!" the biggest goblin agreed instantly. He grabbed the water from Kirsty and began gulping it down.

Rachel handed her bottle to the smallest goblin, who took a long drink.

"My turn!" the big-eared goblin hollered, snatching it from him.

A few moments later the goblins finished drinking and, looking much happier, they gave the bottles back to the girls.

"Now let's go and find some meerkats!" the biggest goblin shouted.

"Wait!" Kirsty said firmly, "What about our deal? You promised us your little toy meerkat."

"We can't give it to you," the biggest goblin snapped. "No way! We need it to catch a meerkat for Jack Frost."

"He'll be very angry with us if we don't bring him one for his zoo!" the smallest goblin added.

Rachel and Kirsty exchanged frustrated glances.

"I told you, there *aren't* any meerkats in the desert," Kirsty said. "You're wasting your time."

The goblins looked uncertain.

"Maybe she's right," the biggest goblin murmured. "After all, we haven't seen any meerkats yet and we've been walking for *hours!*"

"I don't think you're looking in the right place," Rachel remarked, straight-faced. "Don't you know meerkats are *cats*? They've probably climbed those trees to hide!" She pointed at the trees in the distance.

"Yes, *everyone* knows meerkats are cats!" the smallest goblin sneered.

The girls tried not to smile.

"Come on!" the big-eared goblin yelled, and the three of them hurried off towards the trees.

"Well done, girls," Mara whispered from under Kirsty's hat. "You've got them away from the meerkats. Now let's follow them and try to get my key ring back."

But just then the biggest goblin accidentally caught his foot in one of the meerkat holes. He gave a loud yelp and tripped over, ending up flat on his face. Then a horrified Kirsty saw Missy peep out of another hole very close to the fallen goblin.

"Oh no!" Kirsty murmured anxiously.

The girls flapped their hands at Missy, trying to warn her to keep out of sight. They didn't want to call out and attract the goblins' attention.

But the biggest goblin had already spotted the baby meerkat. His eyes lit up.

"Come back!" he yelled to the other goblins, who were ahead of him. "I've found a meerkat!"

Rachel and Kirsty were dismayed as the other two goblins scurried back to join their friend. But before they reached him, Missy popped out of sight again. The girls breathed heartfelt sighs of relief.

"Where's the meerkat?" the smallest goblin panted.

"It was *there*!" The biggest goblin pointed at the hole.

The other goblins frowned.

"That hole's empty," the smallest goblin snorted. "I think you're seeing things! This hot sun can play tricks on your brain, you know."

"He hasn't got a brain!" the goblin with huge ears chortled.

"That's not funny!" the biggest goblin snarled, looking angry.

Then Rachel and Kirsty saw a flash of brown fur inside a different hole very close by. Missy peeked out of it and stared at the goblins right in front of her.

"Oh no!" Rachel groaned. "The silly goblins are bound to catch little Missy this time!"

But the goblins were still arguing about whether the biggest goblin had seen a meerkat or not, and they didn't notice that there was, in fact, one right under their noses! Then, as the girls watched, Missy sneaked out of the hole and grabbed Mara's magical key ring right out of the biggest goblin's pocket.

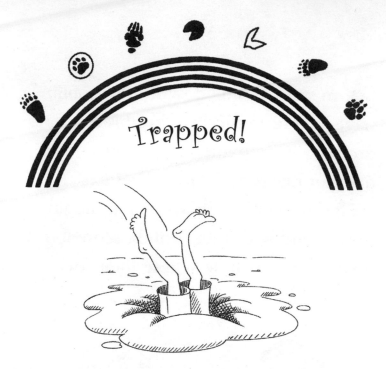

Trapped!

The girls could hardly believe their eyes.

"Missy, bring the toy to us!" Kirsty called. But Missy immediately vanished down the hole again.

The biggest goblin shrieked with rage. "Give that back, you naughty meerkat!" he shouted, and he dived head first into the hole. He disappeared up to his feet, but then stopped.

"I'm stuck upside down!" the goblin
screeched furiously, waving his feet
around. "Come and dig me out – and
get that meerkat for Jack Frost!"

The two other goblins began digging
in the sand with their hands, scooping it
away from the hole where their friend
was stuck.

"Can you see the meerkat?" the
smallest goblin cried.

"No!" the biggest goblin roared. "There are lots and lots of tunnels down here. It's like a maze. Keep digging!"

Mara flew out from under Kirsty's hat. "I'll turn you into fairies, girls, and then we can fly through the tunnels and find Missy," she told them.

One flick of Mara's wand sent glittering fairy sparkles spinning all around Rachel and Kirsty, shrinking them down to fairy-size with delicate fairy wings on their backs. Then Mara shot away towards a nearby hole, and Rachel and Kirsty whizzed after her.

"You know animals love our magical key rings," Mara reminded the girls as they entered the hole. "So we *must* find Missy and persuade her to give it back to me. Come on, girls!"

But the instant Mara, Rachel and Kirsty flew inside the hole, the walls of the tunnel began to shake with a loud noise. *BOOM! BOOM! BOOM!*

"What's that?" Rachel gasped nervously, dodging a clod of earth that fell from the roof of the tunnel. Another clod tumbled down and almost 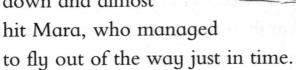 hit Mara, who managed to fly out of the way just in time.

"I think the goblins must be stomping on the ground, trying to drive the meerkats out of their holes," Mara

58

exclaimed. "We *must* find Missy before the tunnels start collapsing!"

Rachel and Kirsty quickly followed Mara down the tunnel, trying to avoid the bits of the roof and walls now falling thick and fast around them. Kirsty couldn't believe how many passageways there were underneath the desert sand. Everywhere she looked, there were more and more tunnels going in lots of different directions.

"How do we know which way to go next?" Kirsty shouted above the noise the goblins were making.

Suddenly the two meerkat guards came scurrying towards them.

"Have you seen Missy?" Rachel asked, looking worried.

"She went that way," one of the

meerkat guards
replied,
pointing down
a nearby
tunnel.

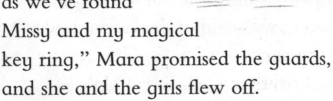

"We'll
deal with the
goblins as soon
as we've found
Missy and my magical
key ring," Mara promised the guards,
and she and the girls flew off.

Suddenly a scared little voice floated
faintly up the tunnel towards them.
"Help! Help!"

"It's Missy!" Mara cried. She flew
faster, Rachel and Kirsty right at her
heels. The three friends zoomed around
the corner of the tunnel, then came to a

dead stop. There in front of them was the upside-down goblin, and they'd almost flown straight into his head which was blocking the tunnel!

Then Rachel exclaimed in dismay. On the other side of the goblin she'd spotted Missy. The baby meerkat, still clutching Mara's key ring, was cowering away from the goblin. And beyond Missy, Rachel could see that the tunnel had fallen in because of the goblins stomping around overhead. Missy couldn't go forwards because of the goblin, and she couldn't go backwards because of the blocked tunnel.

"Missy's trapped!" Rachel cried. "And so is Mara's magical key ring!"

Rabbit Line-up

The upside-down goblin was staring at Mara and the girls.

"Go away!" he shouted. "You can't have that magical key ring — it's mine, and so is this meerkat!"

Missy whimpered in distress.

"Rachel, you help Missy escape," Mara whispered. "Kirsty and I will try to distract the goblin by tickling him!"

Rachel flew as close to the goblin as she dared. "Missy, don't be frightened," she called. "Just come over here to me. You'll be quite safe."

"Don't you dare move!" the goblin screeched at Missy. "I want that magical key ring, and you're coming with me to Jack Frost's zoo!"

"Let's go, Kirsty!" Mara whispered. The two of them zoomed over to the goblin and, fluttering around him, they began tickling his ribs.

"Stop that!" the goblin yelled. "Ha ha, hee hee – no, stop it! Ha ha ha!"

Rachel beckoned to Missy, who came forward cautiously. There was only a small gap between the goblin and the wall of the tunnel, but Missy bravely began squeezing through the small space. Rachel watched, her heart pounding.

But then, just as Missy climbed over the goblin's arm to safety, his hand shot out and he wrenched the magic key ring away from her.

"Your silly plan didn't work!" the goblin gloated triumphantly as Missy scrambled past him to the other side of the tunnel. "I've got the key ring back! Aren't I clever?"

"You're not so clever, really," Kirsty pointed out. "After all, you're still stuck in the sand!"

"But we'll help you out of the hole if

you give us my meerkat key ring back," Mara added.

The goblin's face fell. "So *either* I go back to Jack Frost's Ice Castle without a meerkat, *or* I stay stuck upside down in the desert?" he asked sulkily.

"You decide!" Rachel told him.

The goblin scowled. Then reluctantly he held out the key ring to Mara. "Help me!" he muttered.

Smiling delightedly, Mara touched her magic key ring and it immediately shrank to its Fairyland size. Quickly, Mara clipped it to her belt.

"Come along, girls," she said. "We'll have to go outside again to free the goblin."

The three friends flew back along the tunnels towards the hole, a curious Missy scampering along behind.

"The other goblins have stopped stomping around," Rachel remarked as they flew out of the hole. "I wonder why?" Then she smiled as she saw the two goblins lying exhausted on the sand.

"Look, there's a meerkat," the smallest goblin said wearily, pointing at Missy.

"I don't care!" the goblin with the big ears wailed. "I've never been so hot and tired in my entire life!"

Mara pointed her wand at the biggest goblin's feet, sticking out of the sand. He shot out of the hole backwards, like a ball from a cannon, and landed safely near the other two.

"Poor old goblins!" Mara said. "They look all hot and bothered, don't they?"

She waved her wand again, and the girls saw a pool of clear water, surrounded by tall palm trees, appear a little way off.

"It's an oasis!" the biggest goblin exclaimed. "Hurrah!"

The three goblins raced over to the oasis and began gulping down water in the cool shade. Rachel and Kirsty grinned at each other.

"My magic has repaired all the underground tunnels, too," Mara explained to the girls.

Rachel and Kirsty could now see Missy and the other meerkats popping out of all the holes. "Thank you!" the meerkats squeaked. "Thank you for protecting us."

"And thank *you* for all your help, girls," Mara said. "I couldn't have done it without you. How thrilled they'll be in Fairyland when I give them the good news! And now it's time for you to return to Wild Woods."

"Goodbye, Missy," Rachel and Kirsty called as Mara lifted her wand for the third time. "Goodbye, Mara!"

A mist of fairy sparkles dazzled the girls for a moment. Then they found themselves in the meadow again, human-sized and surrounded by rabbits.

"I have an idea how we can count the

rabbits," Kirsty announced. She checked
to make sure no one was around,
then she turned to a group of bunnies.
"Excuse me," Kirsty said, "would you
mind lining up so we can count you?"

"Of course!" the rabbits agreed, and
they hopped to stand behind each other
in a line. The girls hurried around the
field, asking all the other bunnies to join
them and soon they had a long, long line
winding all around the meadow.

"That was a brilliant idea, Kirsty!" Rachel exclaimed, as they counted the last few rabbits. "Well, that makes fifty-two in total."

"Not quite," Kirsty replied, smiling as a baby bunny scurried over to join the end of the line. "Fifty-three!"

"Thank you, bunnies!" Rachel called, and then the girls saw Becky coming through the woods. The rabbits immediately scattered.

"Just in time!" Kirsty whispered.

"How did you get on, girls?" Becky enquired, coming to join them.

"Oh, we counted a total of fifty-three rabbits in this meadow," Kirsty said confidently, and she and Rachel showed Becky their clipboards.

"Well done, girls," Becky said with

a smile. "I'm impressed. It was a very tricky task – and I really think you deserve your badges!" She handed them a badge each, and the girls were thrilled to see that they had a picture of a rabbit on them.

"Wasn't Missy gorgeous?" Kirsty whispered as she and Rachel followed Becky back to the nature centre.

"She was cuter than cute!"

Rachel whispered back. "And I can't *wait* to find out which animals we'll be meeting tomorrow!"

Now it's time for Kirsty and
Rachel to help...

Savannah the Zebra Fairy

Read on for a sneak peek...

"I wonder which junior ranger badges
we'll earn today," said Rachel Walker as
she got out of the car at the Wild Woods
Nature Reserve.

"I hope we'll be spending time with
the animals again," said her best friend
Kirsty Tate. "Since the fairies gave us
the gift of being able to understand what
animals say, I want to be with them the
whole time!"

The girls smiled at each other happily.
As friends of Fairyland, they were used
to magical adventures. But this summer
they were having a non-magical

adventure too. They were spending a week as volunteer junior rangers at the Wild Woods Nature Reserve. Every day, the junior rangers earned badges for their backpacks by doing jobs around the reserve. Rachel and Kirsty had already earned three badges for their backpacks.

"This week is going so fast," said Rachel. "I can't believe it's already our fourth day!"

"Look, there's Becky," said Kirsty, seeing the head of the reserve walking towards them. "Come on, let's find out what she wants us to do today."

Read Savannah the Zebra Fairy to find out what adventures are in store for Kirsty and Rachel!

Meet the
Baby Animal Rescue Fairies

The Baby Animal Rescue Fairies have lost all their magical
items. But luckily, Kirsty and Rachel are there to
save the day and make sure all baby animals
in the world are safe and sound.

www.rainbowmagicbooks.co.uk

Look out for the next sparkly
Rainbow Magic Special!

Robyn the Christmas Party Fairy

Rachel and Kirsty are helping to organise a big Christmas party.
But Jack Frost has stolen Robyn the Christmas Party Fairy's
magical objects! The girls must help Robyn,
before the spirit of Christmas is lost forever...

Out now!

RAINBOW magic

Meet the fairies, play games
and get sneak peeks at
the latest books!

www.rainbowmagicbooks.co.uk

There's fairy fun for everyone on
our wonderful website.
You'll find great activities, competitions, stories and
fairy profiles, and also a special newsletter.

Get 30% off all Rainbow Magic books at

www.rainbowmagicbooks.co.uk

Enter the code RAINBOW at the checkout.
Offer ends 31 December 2013.

Offer valid in United Kingdom and Republic of Ireland only.

Competition!

The Baby Animal Rescue Fairies have created
a special competition just for you!
In the back of each book in the series there will be
a question for you to answer.
Once you have collected all the books and all
seven answers, go online and enter the competition!

We will put all the correct entries into a draw and select
a winner to receive a special Rainbow Magic Goody Bag,
featuring lots of treats for you and your fairy friends.
The winner will also star in a new Rainbow Magic story!

**What type of dancing does
Saskia the Dance Fairy like?**

_ _ _ _ _

Enter online now at www.rainbowmagicbooks.co.uk

No purchase required. Only one entry per child.
Two prize draws will take place on 1st April 2014 and 2nd July 2014. Alternatively readers can
send the answer on a postcard to: Rainbow Magic, Baby Animal Rescue Fairies Competition,
Orchard Books, 338 Euston Road, London, NW1 3BH. Australian readers can write to:
Rainbow Magic, Baby Animal Rescue Fairies Competition, Hachette Children's Books,
level 17/207 Kent St, Sydney, NSW 2000. E-mail: childrens.books@hachette.com.au.
New Zealand readers should write to:
Rainbow Magic, Baby Animal Rescue Fairies Competition,
4 Whetu Place, Mairangi Bay, Auckland, NZ

Meet the
Rainbow Fairies

Also available as an ebook

Collect the seven original Rainbow Fairies
to find out how the adventure began!

www.rainbowmagicbooks.co.uk